CACTUS JOE'S COWBOY CAPER

By Sam Hay

Illustrated by Daron Parton

W
FRANKLIN WATTS
LONDON • SYDNEY

CHAPTER 1

One wild windy Wednesday, the tumbleweeds
blew into town. Up – down – round and
round. The tumbleweeds bounced off
buildings and raced along roads.

Everyone in Prickly Plains stayed indoors. Everyone apart from Cactus Joe and his best friend, Little Bo, who were playing dodgeball with the weeds.

"Wheee!" Cactus Joe shouted, jumping high. "Yeeeh-ha!" Little Bo shouted, dodging low. They chased and raced. They jumped and bumped.

Then...WHOOOOOOSH! An enormous tumbleweed appeared. "Watch out!" Cactus Joe shouted. But it was too late. "Help!" Little Bo yelled. "I can't get out!" The weed had crashed into Little Bo and swallowed her whole. Its dangly, tangly roots trapping her inside.

Cactus Joe tried to catch the weed, but it bounced away with Little Bo stuck inside. "Don't worry, Little Bo," Cactus Joe called. "I'll get you out!" But every time he got close, the wind blew harder and the weed bounced higher.

The giant tumbleweed rolled up the street and past the Desert Diner...

...past the Happy Hat Store...

...and right past the Big Rock Cinema!

"S-s-s-t-o-p!" Cactus Joe panted. But the weed just rolled further and further away, until it disappeared into the desert.

CHAPTER 2

Cactus Joe scratched his hat. "Bother my boots and spurs!" he said. "How am I going to rescue Little Bo?" Then an idea popped into his head. Of course! Magic cactus juice!

Cactus Joe's uncle made the most amazing magic juice from the cacti that grew in his garden. One swig and the juice gave you special powers. The only trouble was, you never knew exactly what those special powers would be. Sometimes the juice made you tall. Really tall!

Sometimes it made you small. So small you could ride a beetle!

And sometimes it made you invisible – well, almost.

Cactus Joe ran all the way to Uncle Mo's shack. "Uncle Mo! Uncle Mo!" Cactus Joe panted. "Little Bo's got stuck in a terrible tumbleweed. I need some magic cactus juice to rescue her!" Uncle Mo scratched his chin. "A terrible tumbleweed, you say? Right, let's go and find some cactus juice, quickly!"

Uncle Mo led the way to shelves full of
hundreds of bottles of cactus juice.

"Wow," said Cactus Joe. "There are so many
bottles! Which one should we choose?"

"This one, I think," Uncle Mo said, picking up a small bottle.

"Mmm," Cactus Joe said, glugging it down. "It tastes so sweet!" But then Cactus Joe felt a wiggle, and a jiggle, and his feet started to flip-flap on the floor.

"Uh-oh!" said Cactus Joe.

"You drank goose juice!" Uncle Mo said with a chuckle. "Perfect for catching a runaway tumbleweed!"

Cactus Joe began to waddle-walk around Uncle Mo's shack. Flip-flap, flip-flap! His feet got faster. Flip-flap, flip-flap!

Then his arms joined in too – flapping like wings. Flap-pat, flap-pat, flap-pat. He tried to speak and let out a loud "HONK!"

Cactus Joe waddled out of the front door, getting faster and faster. Flip-flap, flip-flap, went his feet. Flap-pat, flap-pat, went his arms.

He grew more feathers. His feet got bigger. And something odd was happening to his nose…"A beak?" he tried to say but all he heard was a "Honk, honk!"

"Don't fly too high!" Uncle Mo shouted as Cactus Joe suddenly took off – up, up into the air! The wind caught his wings, lifting him higher and higher. Too high! Cactus Joe's tummy did a loop-the-loop! In seconds, Uncle Mo and his shack looked like teeny-tiny ants, far, far below.

Cactus Joe swooped and soared through the clouds. "C-A-W!" A giant eagle appeared. It looked hungry! Cactus Joe flew into a cloud to hide. Then he heard a shout from way down below. It was Little Bo!

CHAPTER 4

Cactus Joe poked his head out of the cloud. The eagle had gone. He soared down low. He spotted the giant tumbleweed with Little Bo still trapped inside, bouncing across the desert. Uh-oh! It was heading for Bison Creek – the most dangerous place in Prickly Plains! All the wild bison grazed there!

WHOOSH! The wind blew harder, and the giant tumbleweed took off even faster – heading straight for the bison!

"Watch out, Little Bo!" Cactus Joe tried to shout. But it came out as "HONK! HONK, HONK, HONK!"

The bison snorted. They tossed their heads. They pounded the ground with their big hairy legs! And they charged right at the tumbleweed!

CHAPTER 5

"H-O-N-K!" Cactus Joe had to do something, or Little Bo would be squished like a fly! Cactus Joe swooped low and grabbed the giant tumbleweed with his goosey feet.

SCHLOOP! Just in time!

"Cactus Joe?" Little Bo peeped out of the weed. "Is that you?"

"HONK!" Cactus Joe replied. He had to flap really hard to lift the heavy weed.

He flew towards Uncle Mo's shack. But as he got close he felt a tingle. "Uh-oh!" Cactus Joe thought. "The goose juice is wearing off!" His feathers began to disappear. His feet began to shrink and when he honked, real words came out.

"AHHHH!" Cactus Joe yelled.

"AHHHH!" Little Bo shouted.

Down, down, down they fell...

...until PRANG! The tumbling tumbleweed suddenly stopped, spiked on a large prickly cactus. DONK! Cactus Joe crashed on top!

Now Cactus Joe and Little Bo were both
swallowed whole, trapped inside the tangly,
dangly tumbleweed's roots, pinned to the
giant cactus.

Just then Uncle Mo appeared.

"Hi kids! I guess the goose juice worked!

So what are you two going to do now?"

Uncle Mo asked. "How about playing some

more dodgeball?"

"No way!" said Cactus Jo and Little Bo.

"Too much bouncing," said Little Bo, rubbing her bruises.

"Too much flapping," Cactus Joe said, stretching his arms. Not to mention that their clothes were full of prickles – ouch!

Franklin Watts
First published in Great Britain in 2015 by
The Watts Publishing Group

SERIES EDITOR: Melanie Palmer
SERIES ADVISOR: Catherine Glavina
COVER DESIGN: Cathryn Gilbert
DESIGN MANAGER: Peter Scoulding

ISBN 978 1 4451 4282 1 (hbk)
ISBN 978 1 4451 4283 8 (pbk)
ISBN 978 1 4451 4284 5 (library ebook)

Printed in China

Franklin Watts
An imprint of
Hachette Children's Group
Part of The Watts Publishing Group
Carmelite House
50 Victoria Embankment
London EC4Y 0DZ

An Hachette UK Company
www.hachette.co.uk

www.franklinwatts.co.uk